AbbeyLoo is a curious little girl with a BIG imagination. This imagination takes AbbeyLoo to some very exciting and often unexpected places.

AbbeyLoo loves exploring her backyard. There is always something new to see. Her favorite find is the many toads that roam there. AbbeyLoo loves to carefully catch the toads and pet them and talk to them. Normally they don't talk back, but today is totally different. Follow along with AbbeyLoo on her latest adventure as she meets Gus the Talking Toad

Published by Waldorf Publishing

2140 Hall Johnson Road
#102-345
Grapevine, Texas 76051
www.WaldorfPublishing.com

The Amazing Adventures of AbbeyLoo

AbbeyLoo and Gus the Talking Toad

ISBN: 9781943274383
Library of Congress Control Number: 2015935552

Printed in the United States of America

The Adventures of AbbeyLoo

AbbeyLoo and Gus the Talking Toad

by Tammy Cortez

AbbeyLoo is an inquisitive little girl with a fun and often wild imagination. She can always turn a boring day into a fun filled adventure. Her backpack filled with the necessary tools for exploration, AbbeyLoo sets out each day to find a new adventure.

AbbeyLoo's backyard is a fun place to play. With her big imagination, she often imagines her yard to be a far-off place, creating a new adventure for her every day. There are lots of trees and rocks to climb on and explore. There are flowerbeds that attract butterflies and hummingbirds. There are places around the yard where sprinkler water collects and becomes pools for a happy toad or a bird, and even the occasional dragonfly, to get a drink or a dip when passing by. To her, this backyard is a magical place full of fantasy and great adventure.

One warm, sunny day, AbbeyLoo was out exploring her backyard and came across a toad wandering around. There are many toads that roam around her yard. However, this toad was larger than the toads she normally came across. Excited and very curious, AbbeyLoo snuck up on the toad and grabbed it as she often did when she saw toads in the yard. There was something about the toads who roamed her yard that always intrigued her.

As AbbeyLoo grabbed the toad, he let out a loud, "Hey! What do you think you are doing human?"

AbbeyLoo was in shock and she dropped the toad immediately to the ground and jumped backward. The toad screeched, "Ouch! Why did you have to go and do that?"

AbbeyLoo stood there looking at the toad for a moment, then crept up softly and squatted down.

She looked at the toad and whispered, "You can talk?"

The toad grumpily replied, "Yes I can talk!"

AbbeyLoo, still amazed by this discovery, asked the toad "What is your name?"

The annoyed toad replied, "My name is Gus."

AbbeyLoo smiled and said, "Hello Gus, my name is AbbeyLoo. It is very nice to meet you." She then asked, "Do all of the toads talk or are you a special toad?"

Gus then hopped up onto a rock and replied, "Though I like to consider myself something special, we do all talk. Normally humans can't understand us they just hear croaking. I am confused why you can understand me."

Equally confused by it all, AbbeyLoo replied, "I have no idea. All I normally hear is croaking out here."

AbbeyLoo thought for a minute and realized that she had spilled a jar of magic fairy dust when she was pretending that it would give her the power to understand animals when they talked.

"Maybe that fairy dust was real after all!" AbbeyLoo exclaimed.

Gus looked at her confused so AbbeyLoo sat down next to Gus and explained the whole thing to him.

"You see, one day I was given two jars of magic fairy dust. Normally this stuff is just sparkly dust and doesn't do anything other than make a mess. But yesterday, I was out here and pretending that it was really magical and would allow me to understand all of the creatures out in the yard when they talked."

Gus said, "That has to be it! What else can explain this?"

AbbeyLoo agreed. There really wasn't any other explanation.

Gus then asked AbbeyLoo "What is your fascination with us toads anyway? I always see you picking us up."

AbbeyLoo replied "I just think you are all so cute and you all are so different. I like to get a good look at everyone when I see them. I do not want to hurt anyone, you all are just very interesting."

With a sigh of relief, Gus smiled and said, "Oh, yes. We are all very different. However it can be scary to be caught and placed in containers."

AbbeyLoo looked at Gus and said, "Oh... well... um... I am very sorry about that. I will not pick any of you up again. I would never want to frighten anyone."

AbbeyLoo had lots of questions for Gus. She wanted to know how long their tongues were, what their homes looked like, why they croaked mostly at night and what they were saying. Gus could barely keep up with her.

Suddenly, AbbeyLoo's mom called her in for dinner. "AbbeyLoo, It's time for dinner. Come in and wash up!" her mother called out.

AbbeyLoo turned to Gus and said, "I am sorry Gus, but I have to go eat dinner. I can come back out tomorrow after school and we can talk more. Can you meet me here at this same spot?"

Gus agreed to meet her in that very spot and that he would let the others know that she was of no harm to them. AbbeyLoo ran off to dinner very excited for tomorrow.

She was so excited that she could barely eat her dinner. Her mother noticed that something was on her mind and asked, "AbbeyLoo, what is on your mind? You are not eating much and are abnormally quiet."

AbbeyLoo knew she could never tell her mom about the toad and how she could now understand them, so she had to think quickly. "Um... well... I was just thinking about... um... this fun game we have planned for lunch recess tomorrow."

"Really, what game is that?" her mother asked.

"Well, we are going to make up a better version of four square," AbbeyLoo quickly replied.

"What are you doing to change it?" her dad asked.

"Well we aren't totally sure yet. We are still figuring it out. But it will be fun, and tomorrow we will finish making up the new game", she replied.

"Well that sounds like fun. I can't wait to hear what you kids come up with," her dad said.

"Can I be excused now? I want to go to my room and work on some ideas for the game" AbbeyLoo asked.

"You need to finish your dinner then you can go," her mom said. So Abbey-Loo gulped down her dinner, put her plate in the sink, kissed her mom on the cheek and ran off to her room. "Boy, now that was a record!" exclaimed her dad. AbbeyLoo's mom said, "Yes it was. I have never seen her so quiet and distracted at dinner. This must be some game they have going on tomorrow."

The next day, as soon as AbbeyLoo was done with her homework, she rushed outside and returned to the spot where she promised to meet Gus. As she had hoped, he was there waiting for her. They talked and laughed for quite a while. She learned that the toads' lived underground, and that there were miles and miles of tunnels under her own yard where all of the toads lived, in their own little houses and neighborhoods.

Intrigued with what she was learning, she asked if she could go with him and visit his home some day.

Gus said, "AbbeyLoo you are too big to fit into our tunnels."

AbbeyLoo frowned. It was true. She was too big. She thought long and hard and remembered that she had another can of magic fairy dust.

She told Gus, "Maybe if I get the other can of fairy dust, sprinkle it on myself and wish to be small for a day, I would shrink down small enough to fit in the tunnels and come see your world."

Gus said, "You know, that may just work AbbeyLoo."

Since it was getting late, they agreed that AbbeyLoo would meet him in the same place and at the same time tomorrow and she would try out her fairy dust. If that worked, Gus would take her below-ground and show her around.

AbbeyLoo met Gus at the same place with her magic fairy dust. She then sprinkled some magic fairy dust on top of her head, closed her eyes, and as she spun around she said "I wish I was small enough to go visit Gus's underground home."

When she opened her eyes, she was just the right size to fit in the underground world. AbbeyLoo was so happy she was jumping up and down.

Gus then led her to the entrance to where the toads live. As they climbed down the tunnel and entered Gus's town, Abbey's eyes grew as big as saucers.

Gus looked at her and smiled. "Welcome to Hopville." AbbeyLoo smiled as she looked around.

Gus then said, "Just stick with me. I don't know how the others are going to react to having a human down in our world, no matter how small you are."

AbbeyLoo agreed to stay by his side as they walked into this amazingly colorful world.

Once inside, Gus picked up a bright yellow jacket and hat from a coat rack and put them on.

AbbeyLoo looked at him in amazement and asked, "You wear clothes?"

Gus responded, "Of course we do, but only down here. If we wore them above ground, humans would find it alarming. So we leave them down here on our way out."

AbbeyLoo also noticed that Gus was walking on his hind legs now as well. It was all so fascinating. In fact, all of the toads were walking on their hind legs and dressed in colorful clothing. The lady frogs were in beautiful dresses with floppy hats. Their children were wearing brightly colored clothing as well.

"It is like spring down here," she whispered.

Gus smiled and said, "Yes it is. We have spring all year long in our world."

As the two strolled around this amazing place, AbbeyLoo saw beautiful flowers and sparkling rocks everywhere. The toads lived and worked in brightly colored mushrooms.

It is so magical down here, she thought.

Gus turned to Abbey and said, "I bet you didn't expect it to look like this, did you?"

AbbeyLoo replied softly, "No I didn't. It is amazing!"

Gus just smiled and said, "Come along. I will show you my home and you can meet my family. Then I can show you around some more."

Baked Bug Bakery
Pharmacy
Café
Beauty Salon &SPA
TOWN SQUARE
WEST HOPVILLE
Uptown

Gus led AbbeyLoo along a colorful stone walkway to a big beautiful mushroom. "This is it", Gus said, "What do you think?"

AbbeyLoo looked at him and said, "It is beautiful! I wish my home looked like this. It is so bright and cheerful."

Gus's house was bright yellow with a purple roof. It had a big orange door and the front yard was full of colorful flowers and a well-trimmed lawn with a white picket fence running around it. The green grass in his yard was brighter than any other grass she had ever seen. The colorful flowers were so bright and smelled better than any flowers she had ever smelled before.

Buster

Gus and Millies's home

Gus led her into his home where she met his wife Millie and two kids Billy and Rosie. They were all so friendly and welcoming. AbbeyLoo was still amazed that she could understand all of the toads as they spoke.

They had a pet beetle named Buster. AbbeyLoo couldn't help but giggle when she was introduced to Buster. It was a funny thought after all, a beetle as a pet? Who would have thought of such a thing?

Millie made them all a cup of tea and they sat down and enjoyed it together. AbbeyLoo learned more about their family and their lives underground.

AbbeyLoo asked Gus and Millie, "What kind of work do you do? Do you all have jobs?"

Gus replied, "I own the hat shop in town. We make hats of all shapes and sizes and in bright colors and fun prints. If you would like, we can go down and see my hat shop after tea and I can show you around the town a bit more."

AbbeyLoo replied, "I would like that very much."

Millie told AbbeyLoo that she was a teacher. AbbeyLoo was so excited and told Millie how she hoped to be a teacher when she grew up as well. Abbey-Loo asked Gus's kids about their school. Rosie and Billy told her everything.

"We learn to read, spell and write. We also do mathematics. We have classes on sewing, cooking, building and hunting. Everyone has a job in our world and our school teaches us how to do our best at that job," Billy explained.

Millie told Abbey that they even have sports such as track and field, swimming, and diving. They also have activities such as band and student council.

Rosie told Abbey, "I am one of the best divers on my schools dive team and also class president. Billy is a high jumper and plays the trombone."

They were so excited to tell AbbeyLoo all about their school and activities and AbbeyLoo was equally excited to hear all about them. Rosie and Billy wanted to know about Abbeys school as well. They spent quite a while comparing their schools and what they learned.

As they were sharing great stories about their lives, someone pounded on Gus's door. It was several of the toads from around town. They wanted to know who he had hiding in his home.

"I don't have anyone hiding in my home guys. But I do have a new friend AbbeyLoo that is visiting for the day," Gus told them.

"Who is this AbbeyLoo? We heard you had a human in here," they asked.

Gus then said, "Yes I do have a human. But she is OK, and a friend. She is not here to hurt anyone. She is eager to learn about our world." They were not happy with this at all.

Gus continued, "I think if we share this with her, she will do a good job at helping us maintain a safe place to roam above ground."

They demanded to speak with her at once. After all AbbeyLoo was what they called a "Toad Hunter." All humans were considered this, especially the younger ones. AbbeyLoo was scared to face them.

With Millie's encouragement, she was brave and went to talk with them. She sat down and explained herself to them and promised to never pick them up again. They said they would allow her to stay and visit but they insisted that she sign a Peace Treaty with them. If not she had to leave at once and could never come back. AbbeyLoo was handed the paper and she read it.

The Peace Treaty said, "I _____ will not hunt, pick up, contain, or disturb the toads as they roam the above ground world that I live in ever again. I will also stop others from doing so as well. I will respect that the toads serve a purpose above ground and I will do all that I can to make sure that they can do their jobs safely."

AbbeyLoo filled in her name and happily signed the treaty and they shook hands.

Then Gus and his family invited her to join them in the town square for the parade and festival.

AbbeyLoo said, "Ooh a parade? I love parades!" and happily accepted their invitation

As they walked to the center of town, Gus, Millie, Billy, and Rosie pointed out shops, restaurants, the school and other things to AbbeyLoo. As they passed Gus's shop they stopped and went in to take a peek. It was a fun store full of beautiful hats.

There were hats for men, women and children. They were all brightly colored and had fun details added to them. The ones with flowers and butterflies were her favorite.

"I wish I had hats like this to wear," she told Gus.

He said "If I could make one big enough for you I would."

Millie asked Gus if he could give Abbey one of the hats he made as a keepsake. Gus agreed and let AbbeyLoo pick her favorite hat to take home. AbbeyLoo chose a bright yellow hat with a green and white polka dot band around it.

Baby Bonnets

Gus's Hat Shack

They left the hat shop and continued their walk to the center of town. When AbbeyLoo got to the center of town she was surprised to see the little toads playing in the park on a jungle gym and toads walking their pet beetles to the Beetle Park to let them play. There were shops and cafés all over the place. Toads could be seen sitting out on café tables having tea and catching up with their friends. They were picnicking in the park and playing Frisbee. There were younger toads playing hopscotch on the blacktop. It was a lot like home but so much more amazing to look at.

Just as she was taking it all in, the mayor of Hopville could be seen walking up to the podium to make the opening announcements for the parade and festival. As he arrived, two toads with trumpets standing next to the podium played a song to signal his arrival and for everyone to gather around. The mayor was tall and wore a bright red coat and red and green striped top hat. He carried a cane and had a giant smile. At the podium the Mayor raised his hands and welcomed everyone to the festival. Everyone cheered and clapped.

Once the mayor was done with his opening announcements, a marching band came down the street and circled around the center of town. Toads danced along and clapped with the music. AbbeyLoo couldn't help but join in and dance herself.

There were acrobatic toads and toads dressed like clowns blowing bubbles and doing tricks as they paraded through town.

There was even a toad with a rolling cart selling Frozen Flysicles, which Abbey-Loo declined, of course, but the little toads seemed to really enjoy them.

There was also a man selling cotton candy made out of brightly colored spider webs.

In one of the parks next to the center of town, there was a carnival with rides and games. They had a merry go-round but instead of horses and other animals as AbbeyLoo was used to seeing, they were riding on different kinds of bugs, like beetles, butter flies and dragon flies. They had a Ferris Wheel and a rollercoaster. It looked a lot like the fairs AbbeyLoo had been to with her family.

AbbeyLoo turned to Gus and said, "Your world is so much fun!" She giggled and tried to take in as much of the fun as possible. She even went on a rollercoaster ride with Billy and Rosie.

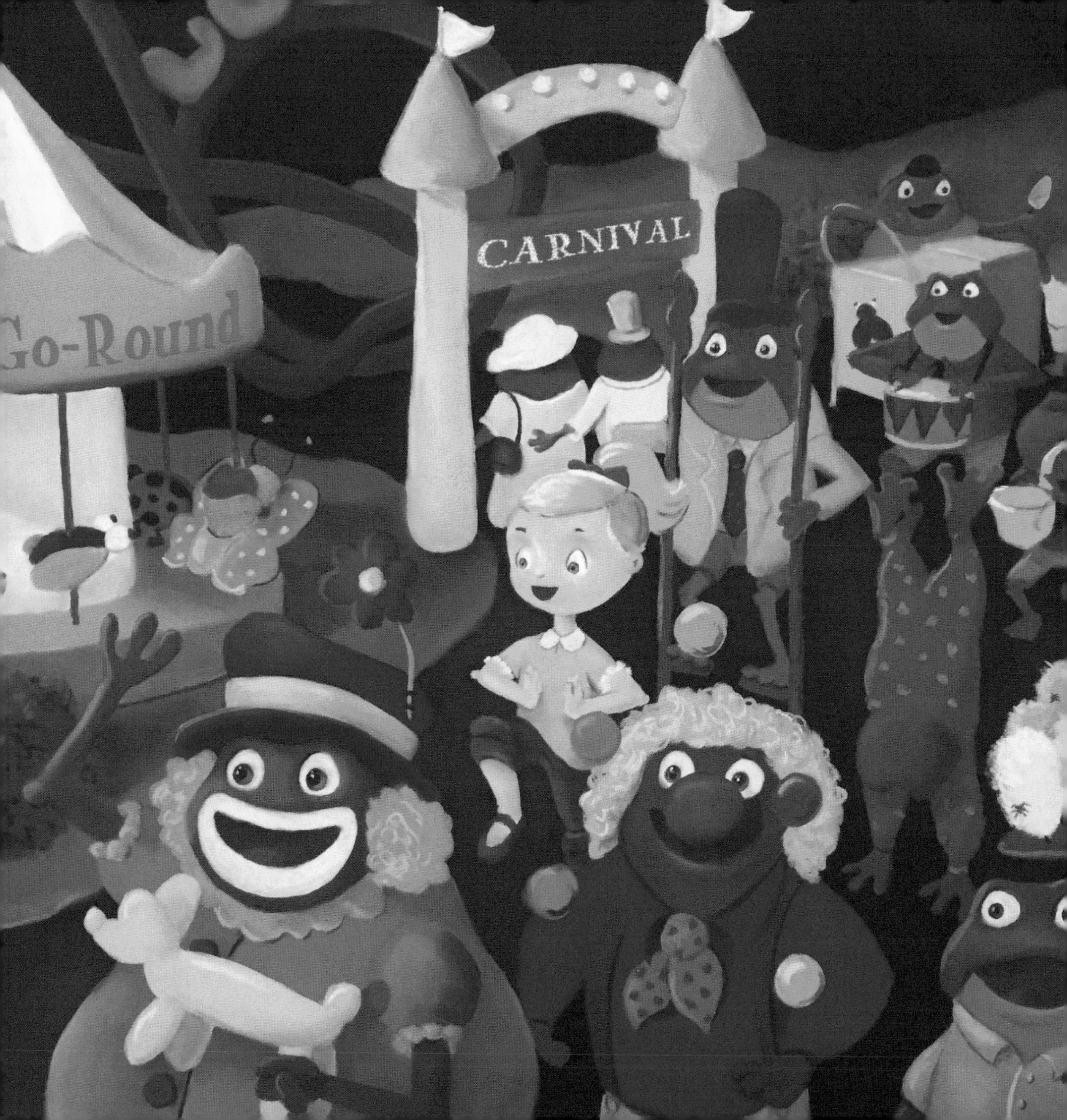
Go-Round
CARNIVAL

Realizing she had been down there for quite some time, AbbeyLoo looked at her watch and realized that her mother would soon be looking for her for dinner. So she thanked everyone for their kindness and said goodbye. Millie, Billy and Rosie all gave AbbeyLoo a hug and thanked her for visiting. Gus walked her back to the exit so she could head back home.

He said, "Thank you AbbeyLoo for coming to visit today and for signing the Peace Treaty. We are grateful to have a human friend like you. Please come again, anytime."

AbbeyLoo thanked him for the wonderful day and headed up the hole.

No clothes beyond this point
Human ahead

As AbbeyLoo climbed up the tunnel, she was so grateful for the wonderful day she had. It was a day she would never, ever forget. Once she got back above ground, she took some of her magic fairy dust in her hand and made a wish to be big again, then sprinkled it on top of her head and spun around. When she opened her eyes, she was back to her normal size again. She looked around, with a little laugh she skipped back to her house, putting her magic fairy dust in a safe place for later and the hat she picked out at Gus's shop on her night stand.

AbbeyLoo couldn't wait to visit Hopville again.

Author Bio

Tammy Cortez is a Northern California native now living in Central Texas. Being a mother to two girls she is always finding creative inspiration through them. Whether it is through cooking, decorating, crafting, photography or writing Tammy is always being inspired to create. She originally wrote this story as a gift for her youngest daughter, but after discussing it with a couple of friends she was convinced she should publish it. Tammy first found her love of writing when she was in high school through a fun writing exercise her English teacher did with them. This exercise was intended to produce a couple of pages, but typically resulted in Tammy writing 6+ pages by the time it was complete. Writing this book brought her love of writing back to life.

Dedication

This book is dedicated to my two beautiful daughters, Kylie and Abbey, who have shown me the true meaning of unconditional love and for never allowing me to forget how important and powerful embracing your imagination is. You are my greatest creations and the core of my heart and soul!

A big, big thank you to my husband and rock of 25 years for always loving and supporting me. Also to my parents who taught me so much but most importantly that character is everything. You all are the reason I am who I am.